MW01154621

VOLUME TWO

VOLUME TWO

WHITNEY G.

Copyright © 2014 by Whitney Gracia Williams

Cover designed by Najla Qambers of Najla Qambers Designs
http://najlaqamberdesigns.com/

ISBN: 1500409111
ISBN 13: 9781500409111

For my BFF/ultimate beta-reader/amazing assistant/shoulder to cry on whenever I'm acting crazy/ "person" like they say on 'Grey's Anatomy'...Tamisha Draper.

My books would suck without you...

And for the F.L.Y. crew...

table of contents

prologue

Andrew

New York City
Six years ago...

For the third week in a row, I woke up to a relentless rain falling over this repulsive city. The clouds above were coated in an ugly hue of grey, and the streaks of lightning that flashed across the sky every few seconds were no longer marvels; they were predictable.

Holding up my umbrella, I walked to a newspaper stand and picked up *The New York Times*—bracing myself for what lay between its pages.

"How many women do you think a man could possibly screw in his lifetime?" The vendor asked as he handed me my change.

"I don't know," I said. "I've stopped counting."

"Stopped counting, eh? What did you do, get to ten and decide that was enough before settling down?" He pointed to the gold band on my left hand.

"No. I settled down first, then I started fucking."

He raised his eyebrow—looking stunned, and then he turned around to organize his cigar display.

A couple of months ago, I would've entertained his attempt to make conversation, would've answered his question with a lighthearted laugh and a "More than we'll ever admit to," but I didn't have the ability to laugh anymore.

My life was now a depressing reel of repeated frames—hotel nights, cold sweats, marred memories, and rain.

Goddamn rain.

I tucked the newspaper underneath my arm and turned away, glancing at the ring on my hand.

I hadn't worn it in a long time, and I had no idea what possessed me to put it on today. Twisting it off my finger, I looked at it one last time—shaking my head at its uselessness.

For a split second, I considered keeping it, maybe locking it away as a reminder of the man I used to be. But that version of me was pathetic—*gullible*, and I wanted to forget him as fast as I could.

I crossed the street as the light turned green, and as I stepped onto the sidewalk, I tossed the band where I should've thrown it months ago.

Down the drain.

exculpatory evidence (n.):

Evidence indicating that a defendant
did not commit the crime.

Andrew

Present Day

The hot coffee that was currently seeping through my pants and stinging my skin was the exact reason why I never fucked the same woman twice.

Wincing, I took a deep breath. "*Aubrey...*"

"You're fucking *married.*"

I ignored her comment and leaned back in my chair. "In the interest of your future short-lived and mediocre law career, I'm going to do two huge favors for you: One, I'm going to apologize for fucking you a second time and let you know that it will *never* happen again. Two, I'm going to pretend like you didn't just assault me with some goddamn coffee."

"*Don't.*" She threw my coffee mug onto the floor, shattering it to pieces. "I definitely did, and I'm tempted to do it again."

"Miss Everhart—"

"*Fuck you.*" She narrowed her eyes at me, adding, "I hope your dick falls off" as she stormed out of my office.

"Jessica!" I stood up and grabbed a roll of paper towels. "*Jessica?*"

No answer.

I picked up my phone to call her desk, but she suddenly stepped into my office. "Yes, Mr. Hamilton?"

"Call Luxury Dry Cleaning and have them deliver one of my suits to the office. I also need a new cup of coffee, Miss Everhart's file from HR, and you need to tell Mr. Bach that I'll be late to that four o'clock meeting today."

I waited to hear her usual "Right away, sir" or "I'm on it, Mr. Hamilton," but she said nothing. She was silent—blushing, and her eyes were glued to the crotch of my pants.

"Don't you need some help cleaning that up?" Her lips curved into a smile. "I have a really thick towel in my desk drawer. It's very soft...and *gentle.*"

"Jessica..."

"It *is* huge, isn't it?" Her eyes finally met mine. "I really wouldn't tell a soul. It would be our little secret."

"My fucking dry cleaning, a new cup of coffee, Miss Everhart's file, and a message to Mr. Bach about me being late. *Now.*"

"I really love the way you resist..." She stole another glance of my pants before leaving the room.

I sighed and started to soak up as much of the coffee as I could. I should've known that Aubrey was the emotional type, should've known that she was unstable and incapable of behaving normally the second I realized she'd made up a fake identity just for LawyerChat.

I regretted ever telling her that I wanted to own her pussy, and I was cursing myself for driving to her apartment yesterday.

Never again...

Just as I was tearing off a new paper towel, a familiar voice cleared the air.

"Why, hello…It's good to see you again," she said.

I lifted my head up, hoping that this was a hallucination—that the woman at my door wasn't really standing there smiling. That she wasn't stepping forward with her hand outstretched as if she wasn't the very reason that my life was heartlessly altered six years ago.

"Are you going to shake my hand, *Mr. Hamilton?*" She raised her eyebrow. "That is the name you're going by these days, isn't it?"

I stared at her long and hard—noticing that her once silky black hair was now cut short into a bob. Her light green eyes were still as soft and alluring as I remembered them, but they weren't having the same effect.

All the memories I'd tried to suppress were suddenly playing right in front of me, and my blood was starting to boil.

"*Mr. Hamilton?*" she asked again.

I picked up my phone. "Security?"

"Are you fucking kidding me?" She slammed the phone down. "You're not going to ask why I'm here? Why I came to see you?"

"Doing so would imply that I *care*."

"Did you know that when most people get sentenced to prison, they get care packages, money orders, even a phone call on their first day?" She clenched her jaw. "I got divorce papers."

"I told you I'd write."

"You told me you'd *stay*. You told me you forgave me, you said that we could start over when I got out, that you would be right there—"

"You fucking ruined me, Ava." I glared at her. "*Ruined me*, and the only reason I said those dumb ass things to you was because my lawyer told me to."

"So, you don't love me anymore?"

"I don't answer rhetorical questions," I said. "And I'm not a geography expert, but I know damn well that North Carolina is outside of New York and a direct violation of your parole. What do you think will happen when they find out you're here? Do you think they'll make you serve out the sentence that you more than fucking deserve?"

She gasped. "You would snitch on me?"

"I would *run my car* over you."

She opened her mouth to say something else, but the door opened and the security team walked in.

"Miss?" The lead guard, Paul, cleared his throat. "We're going to need you to vacate the premises now."

Ava scowled at me. "Really? You're really going to let them haul me off like I'm some kind of animal?"

"Once again, *rhetorical*." I sat down in my chair, signaling for Paul to get rid of her.

She said something else, but I tuned it out. She didn't mean shit to me, and I needed to find someone online tonight so I could fuck her random and unwanted appearance out of my mind.

evasion (n.):

A subtle device to set aside the truth, or
escape the punishment of the law.

Aubrey

A ndrew was the epitome of what it meant to be an asshole, a shining example of what that word stood for, but no matter how pissed I was, I hadn't been able to stop thinking about him.

In the six months that we'd spoken, he'd never mentioned a wife. And the one time I'd asked if he'd ever done anything more than "One dinner. One night. No repeats." –he'd said "Once," and quickly changed the subject.

I'd been replaying that conversation in my mind all night, telling myself to accept that he was a liar, and that I needed to move on.

"Ladies and gentlemen of La Monte Art Gallery..." My ballet instructor spoke into a mic, cutting through my thoughts. "May I have your attention, please?"

I shook my head and looked out into the full audience. Tonight was supposed to be one of the highlights of my dance career. It was an exhibition for the city's college dancers. All of the leading performers for spring productions were supposed to dance a two minute solo in honor of their school, in celebration of what was to come months later.

"This next performer you're about to see is Miss Aubrey Everhart." There was pride in his voice. "She is playing the role of Odette/Odile in Duke's production of *Swan Lake*, and when I tell you that she is one of the most talented dancers I've ever seen..." He paused as the crowd's chatter dissolved into silence. "I need you to take my word for it."

One of the photographers in the front row snapped a picture of me, temporarily rendering me blind by the flash.

"As most of you know," he continued, "I've worked with the best of the best, spent countless years in Russia studying under the greats, and after a long and illustrious career with the New York Ballet Company, I've retired to teach those with untapped potential."

There was a loud applause. Everyone in the room knew who Paul Petrova was, and even though most in the field were confused as to why he'd ever want to teach in Durham, no one dared to question his decision.

"I hope you'll come out and see the first transformation of the Duke ballet program in the spring," he said as he slowly walked to the other side of the stage. "But for now, Miss Everhart will perform a short duet from Balanchine's *Serenade*, with her partner Eric Lofton!"

The audience clapped again, and the lights above them dimmed. A soft spotlight shone on me and Eric, and the violinists began to play.

Short, soft notes filled the room, and I stood on my toes—trying to dance as delicately as the music demanded. Yet, with each step, all I could picture was Andrew kissing me, fucking me, and ultimately *lying* to me.

"I've never lied to you, Aubrey. I trust you for some strange reason..."

I pushed Eric away when he held out his hands, and twirled across the stage until he came after me. He held my face in his hands—as if he was begging me to stay, but I spun away again, launching myself into a full set of nonstop pirouettes.

I was angry, I was hurt, and I wasn't holding anything back as I showed off just how well I could dance en pointe. The second the violinists struck the last note, the audience let out a collective gasp and applauded the loudest they had all night.

"Wow..." Eric whispered as he took a bow next to me. "I don't think anyone will talk shit about you getting the swan role after that..."

"People have been talking shit about me?" I raised my eyebrow, but I already knew the answer to that. A junior landing the top role over all the seniors was unheard of.

"Bravo, Miss Everhart." Mr. Petrova walked over to me. "She's going to blow you all away in the spring, I'm sure of it!"

Another round of applause began to build and he moved the mic away from his mouth. "Where are your parents? I'd like for them to come up for a picture."

"They're out of town." I lied. I hadn't wasted my time even attempting to invite them to this.

"Well, that's too bad," he said. "I'm sure they're very proud of you. You can exit the stage now."

"Thank you." I headed into the dressing room and changed into a short white silk dress and a grey feathered headband. As I looked myself over in the mirror, I smiled. There was no way anyone could tell that I was an emotional wreck inside.

I pulled out my phone and noticed a new voicemail from GBH. I knew it was about me missing my internship for the fourth day in a row, so I deleted it. Then something came over me and I googled "Andrew Hamilton" for the umpteenth time this week—hoping something would pop up.

Nothing. Again.

With the exception of his perfectly poised photo on GBH's website and that less than telling bio, there was no information about him anywhere.

I'd even tried "Andrew Hamilton: New York, lawyer," but the results were just as dismal. It was as if he hadn't come into existence until starting at GBH.

"Great performance, Aubrey…" Jennifer, one of Duke's top seniors, suddenly stepped into the bathroom. "It really is an honor watching someone so young and underdeveloped get unnecessary credit."

I rolled my eyes and zipped my purse.

"Tell me something," she said. "Do you honestly think you're going to last until the spring performance?"

"Do you honestly think I'm going to stand here and continue this dumbass conversation?"

"You should." She smirked. "Because between you and me, four years ago—back before your time…There was a certain dancer picked to be the lead in *Sleeping Beauty*, a double major. She was quite talented—a natural really, but she caved under pressure because she couldn't devote as many hours to the craft as the dancers who only wanted to dance."

"Is there a point to this story?"

"I took her spot and I was only a freshman." She smiled. "Now I'm a senior, and a certain someone is dancing in the role that belongs to me. So, just like back then, I'm going to do everything in my power to make sure I get what's rightfully mine."

I shook my head and moved past her, ignoring the fact that she'd whispered "stupid bitch" under her breath. I was supposed to return to the gallery room and watch the other performers, but I needed a break.

I slipped past the sliding doors on the other side of the room and stepped into the gallery's bistro. It was much quieter on this side, and the people sitting at the tables seemed to be preoccupied with conversations not centered on ballet.

"Miss?" A tuxedoed waiter stepped in front of me with a tray. "Would you be interested in a complimentary glass of champagne?"

"Two, please."

He raised his eyebrow, but handed me two glasses anyway.

With no grace whatsoever, I tossed one back, then the other—licking the rims to make sure I didn't miss a drop.

"Where's your bar?" I asked.

"Our *bar*? I don't think the patrons of the art gallery are permitted to—"

"Please don't make me ask again."

He pointed to the other side of the room where a few smokers were sitting, and I walked toward them.

"What can I get for you tonight, Miss?" The bartender smiled as I approached. "Would you like to try one of our house specials?"

"Can any of those help me forget about sleeping with a married man?"

The smile on his face faded and he set out three shot glasses, filling them with what I could only hope was the strongest liquor in the house.

I slid my credit card across the counter and downed the first one in seconds—shutting my eyes as the burning sensation crawled down my throat. I held the next one against my lips, and I suddenly heard a familiar laugh.

It was low and gravelly, and I'd heard it a million times before.

I turned around and spotted Andrew sitting at a table with a woman who was *not* his wife. I didn't want to admit it, but she was pretty. Very, very pretty: Auburn hair with blond highlights, deep green eyes, and perky breasts that were too perfect to be natural.

She was rubbing him on his shoulder and giggling every ten seconds.

Andrew seemed undaunted by her affection, and as he signaled for the check, I could only assume how their night would end.

I tried to turn away—to act like seeing him with someone else wasn't affecting me, but I couldn't help it.

His date was now leaning over the table—purposely putting more of her cleavage on display, and whispering words that were hard to read. As she playfully licked her lips and stroked his chin with her fingertips, I realized I couldn't take it anymore.

Subject: SERIOUSLY?!
Are you really on a date right now with someone who isn't your wife?! It's bad enough that you're a cheating and lying philanderer, but are you really that much of a sex addict?
—Aubrey

His response came within seconds.

Subject: Re: SERIOUSLY?!
I'm really on a date right now with someone who's not going to leave third degree burns on my dick. And I'm not a sex addict, I'm a pussy addict. There's a difference.
—Andrew

Subject: Re: Re: SERIOUSLY?!
You are a disgusting and vile asshole, and I honestly regret ever sleeping with you.
—Aubrey

No response.

I watched as he looked down at his phone and raised his eyebrow. He turned around in his chair—slowly scanning the room until he found me.

His eyes widened the second they met mine, and his lips slowly parted. His gaze traveled up and down my body, and I could feel him undressing me.

There was suddenly no one else in the room but the two of us and I could tell that he wanted me to come to him—right here, right now. I felt my body responding to his stares, felt my nipples hardening as he dragged his tongue against his lips.

I swallowed as I looked him over, realizing that I'd pictured his hair entirely wrong in my dreams this week. I'd finger fucked myself for hours on end last night—using his face and the memories of his voice for inspiration, and seeing him in person only made me want to feel his cock inside of me again.

I leaned forward, wanting to go to him, but my tunnel vision quickly cleared and I saw that we weren't alone in this room.

Far from it.

His date's perfectly manicured hand found its way to his chin, and turned his head away.

I followed suit and asked for two more drinks. I downed them both and when I looked over my shoulder, I saw that Andrew was staring in my direction with undeniable want in his eyes.

I forced a smile and opened my mouth very slowly, mouthing, "Fuck. You." before leaving. I snatched a handful of mints from a random waiter's tray and rushed back toward the gallery.

I was halfway there when I felt my phone vibrating. An email.

Subject: Meet me in the bathroom.
NOW.
—Andrew

I turned off my phone and continued walking toward the gallery doors—damn near running. I reached the lobby, but someone grabbed my arm and pulled me across the room.

Andrew.

I tried to jerk away, but he tightened his hold and looked back at me—giving me a 'Don't Fuck with Me' look as the people around us whispered.

He pulled me into a bathroom and locked the door, narrowing his eyes at me. "You think I'm disgusting?"

"Extremely." I stepped back. "I've lost what little respect I had for you and if you even *try* to put your hands on me, I'll scream."

"I don't doubt that." A trace of a smile grazed his lips, but it didn't stay. "You haven't shown up to work for four straight days. You think just because I fucked you that I won't fire you?"

"I don't give a fuck whether you fire me or not! Have you ever thought about why I haven't shown up to work?"

"Incompetence?"

"You're fucking married! *Married*! How could you—" I shook my head as he closed the gap between us. "How could you leave that part out?"

"I didn't," he said. "And for the record...I'm not technically married, Aubrey."

"I'm not technically *stupid*, Andrew."

"You're making it very difficult to talk to you right now..." His lips were brushing against mine.

"That's because you're not making any fucking sense." I freed myself from his grasp and headed for the door, but he grabbed me and slammed me against the wall.

"It's a *contested divorce*," he hissed. "If you were a *real* lawyer I'm sure I wouldn't have to explain what the hell that term means, but since you're not—"

"It means that you're still legally married. It means that if you die before the papers go through, that your wife—which is what she is, will still be entitled to everything you ever owned. It means that you're a LIAR! A *fucking liar*, who is apparently exempt from his own stupid and ineffectual rules!"

"I filed." He gritted through his teeth. "She refused to sign, and there's a lot of complicated shit that I'll never feel like discussing, but we've been separated and out of touch for over six years. Six. Years."

I shrugged and tried to put on my best poker face, ignoring the fact that my heart was skipping every other beat as he wiped my tears away with his thumb.

"I've never lied to you, Aubrey," he said sternly. "You asked me before if I'd ever lied to you and that answer is still the same. I don't talk about my life before Durham with anyone, but yes, I did once have a wife and she showed up to my office on her own. I didn't call her, I never will, and I haven't called her since I left New York. Our case is extremely complicated and I prefer not to think about it."

"I don't care," I said. "You're still *wrong*. You still neglected to tell me about her for six months. Six. *Months!*"

"At what point was I supposed to bring that shit up?" His face turned red. "In between fucking you over the phone? When I was begging your lying ass to meet me in person? When I was unknowingly helping you with your fucking *homework*?"

"How about before you fucked me?" I hated that being around him pulled emotions out of me. I couldn't pretend to act unaffected if I tried. "How about then?"

He clenched his jaw, but he didn't say a word.

"That's what I thought," I said, knowing that I'd won this. "Now, I'm sure you and your lovely D-cup date have a room reserved across the street, so if you don't mind—"

"There's nothing going on between me and my soon to be *ex-wife*," he said harshly. "Nothing. And I *do* have a room reserved across the street. I've had the same one reserved for the past four nights with four different women, but I've been unable to fuck any of them because I can't seem to stop thinking about my incompetent-ass-intern and how I only want to fuck her."

Silence.

"Do you…" I shook my head. "Do you honestly think saying shit like that is a turn-on?"

"Yes…" He trailed his fingers underneath my dress, slightly brushing his thumb against the crotch of my soaked panties. "And apparently you do, too…"

"Me being wet just means that I can't control my body's reaction to you. It doesn't mean that I want to have sex with you. I *hate* you."

"I'm pretty sure that you don't." He slipped his hand around my waist and pulled me close—making my breathing slow.

"Get your hands off me…"

"Say it more convincingly and I will." He waited for my request, raising his eyebrow, but I couldn't bring myself to say those words.

We stood staring at each other for several minutes, letting that raw, palpable tension build between us before I finally broke the silence.

"I think you should get back to your date…" My voice was a whisper. "You've said all you had to say so…What more could you possibly want from me?"

"In this moment?" He trailed his finger against my collarbone.

"In general." I turned my cheek before he could kiss me. "I'm never sleeping with you again, I'll be formally resigning by the end of the week, and I think we need to end our so-called friendship for good."

"You mean that?" he whispered.

"Yes, I mean that." I ignored the feel of his hand squeezing my ass. "I want to be friends with someone who's interested in more than my pussy."

"I'm interested in *your mouth,* too."

I had no response for that, and he must've sensed it because he tightened his grip on my waist.

"I know how hard it is for you to tell the truth," he said softly, "so I need you to be completely honest when I ask you these next few questions. Can you do that?"

I nodded, breathlessly, and he leaned closer to my lips. "You don't enjoy fucking me?"

"That's not the issue."

"That's not the *answer*. Tell me."

I ignored the loud beating in my chest. "I do enjoy it…"

"Are you really resigning?" He kissed me.

"No…I just—" I sucked in a breath as his hand cupped my right breast, as he squeezed it. Hard.

"You just *what*?"

"I want to be reassigned to another lawyer, and I don't want to see you any more than I have to."

He stared into my eyes for a long time, not saying a word as he let me go. "That's how you truly feel?"

"Seeing as I'm the only one between us who actually *feels* anything, yes. Yes, that is how I really feel about you."

He blinked. Then he suddenly pulled me back into his arms and crushed his lips onto mine.

"Why are you such a fucking liar, Aubrey?" He hissed. Pushing me against the vanity, he bit down on my bottom lip and snatched the feathered headband out of my hair.

Keeping his lips on mine, he pushed my dress above my waist—ripping off my panties with one pull.

"Andrew…" I tried to catch my breath as he picked me up and set me on the sink. "Andrew, wait…"

"For what?" He grabbed my hand and placed it over his belt, telling me to unbuckle it.

I didn't answer him. I slipped my fingers underneath the metal clip and unclasped it as he pressed his mouth against my neck.

Trailing his tongue against my skin, he whispered, "You haven't missed me fucking you?"

"It was only twice." I sucked in a breath as his hands caressed my thighs. "Not enough to miss anything…"

He bit me harshly and leaned back, glaring at me.

My breath caught in my throat as he slipped two fingers inside my pussy and teasingly moved them in and out.

"It *feels* like you've missed fucking me..." He pushed his fingers as deep as they could go, making me moan.

I arched my back as he stroked my clit with his thumb.

He suddenly pulled his fingers out of me and brought them up to his lips, slowly licking them. "It *tastes* like you've missed fucking me, too." He pressed another finger against my throbbing wet clit and then he brought it up to my face—placing it against my lips. "Open your mouth."

I slowly parted my lips, and he narrowed his eyes as he slid his finger against my tongue. I felt his cock rub against my thigh, felt him using his other hand to wrap my leg around his waist.

"Tell me that you don't want to fuck me," he said. "That you don't want me to bury my cock deep inside of you *right now*."

He grabbed my face and pressed his lips against mine, drawing my bottom lip into his mouth with his teeth.

I was sliding off the edge of the counter, about to fall, but he pressed me back against the mirror.

I kept my eyes locked on his as he unwrapped a condom, as he put it on and stared at me with that same angry expression he'd been wearing all night.

He grabbed me by my ankles and pulled me forward, sliding his cock into me as my legs gripped his waist.

My hands clawed at his neck as he pounded into me again and again.

"*I've* missed fucking you," he rasped, threading his fingers into my hair and pulling my head back. "But you haven't thought about me at all?"

"Ahhh!" I screamed as he sped up his thrusts. I squeezed my legs around him even tighter, trying my best not to give in.

I shut my eyes and heard him saying my name—panting, "Fuck, Aubrey…Fuck…"

"Put your hands on the counter…" he commanded, but I ignored him and tightened my grip around his neck.

"Aubrey…" He bit my shoulder again, still fucking me harder than ever. "Put your hands on the counter. Now."

I slowly unclasped my hands from around him and lowered them to my sides—gripping onto the cold counter. The next thing I felt was his tongue swirling around my nipples, roughly sucking my breasts.

I gripped the tile harder as his kisses became more ravenous—more possessive, and as he fucked me harder and harder, I felt myself on the verge of losing control.

"*Andrew….*" I moaned. "*Andrew….*"

He released my nipple from his mouth and slid his hands underneath my thighs, picking me up and pinning my back against the wall.

"I know you love the way I fuck you, Aubrey…" He looked into my eyes, forcing his cock even deeper into my pussy. "And I know you've touched yourself every night this week, wishing it was my cock inside of you instead of your fingers."

My clit throbbed with his every word, and I was wetter than I'd ever been in my life.

"Tell me it's true…" He pressed his lips against mine and slipped his tongue into my mouth—muffling my moans with an angry, unrelenting kiss. "Finally tell me something that's fucking true…"

Tremors traveled up and down my spine, and I was seconds away from coming, but he wouldn't let my mouth go.

He was still kissing me—glaring at me, begging me to tell him the truth.

I nodded, hoping that he could read my eyes and see that I needed him to let go of me, I needed to be able to breathe.

He slammed into me one last time—hitting my spot, and I managed to tear my mouth away from his.

"Yessssss!" My head fell forward into his shoulder and I gasped for air.

"*Aubrey...*" He gripped my waist until he stopped shaking.

As we both came back down, there were a few random knocks at the door, a few "Is anybody in there?" taps, but both of us remained silent and breathless.

Minutes later, when his breathing seemed to be under control, he pulled out of me—staring into my eyes. He tossed the condom away in the trashcan behind him and pulled up his pants.

I watched as he fixed himself in the mirror, as he smoothed everything so well that no one would ever know that he'd just fucked the shit out of me.

I slid off the sink and looked at my own face—flushed cheeks, wild hair, runny mascara—and pulled my bra straps back over my shoulder. Before I could pull up my dress straps, Andrew moved my hand away and pulled them up for me.

Our eyes met in the mirror as he smoothed my hair, and for a split second he turned away—to pick up my headband. He gently held it over my head and slid it into place, and then he walked away.

"You know, it's rude to just leave someone after sex without saying anything," I muttered.

"What?" His hand was on the doorknob.

"Nothing."

"What did you say?" He cocked his head to the side. "I'm not a mind reader."

"I said it's rude to just leave after you fuck me. You could at least say something, *anything*."

"I don't do pillow talk."

"It's not pillow talk." I scoffed. "It's part of being a gentleman."

"I never said I was a gentleman."

I sighed and turned around. I waited to hear the door close, but his hands were suddenly on my waist and he was spinning me around to face him.

"What am I supposed to say after I fuck you, Aubrey?"

"You could ask if it was good for me or not..."

"I don't believe in asking pointless questions." He looked at his watch. "How long do you have to stay here?"

"Another hour or so."

"Hmmm." He was quiet. "And while you were stalking me and my date how many shots did you have?"

"I wasn't stalking you and your date. I've been avoiding you all week, or haven't you noticed?"

"*How many?*"

"Five."

"Okay." He tucked a strand of hair behind my ear. "I'll take you home whenever you're ready and have someone deliver your car to your apartment tomorrow." He planted a kiss on my forehead before heading to the door. "Just call me."

"Wait," I said as he opened it. "What about your date?"

"What about her?"

———

An hour later, I slipped inside of Andrew's car—a sleek black Jaguar. He held the door open until I was comfortable, and waited until I put on my seatbelt before shutting it.

On his dashboard, I spotted a red folder with a New York State seal on its center. I picked it up, but he immediately took it from me and locked it inside his glove box.

He looked offended that I'd touched it, but he quickly turned away from me and revved up the car.

"Can I ask you something, Andrew?"

"Depends on what it is."

"I googled you this week and nothing came up…"

"That's not a question."

"Why didn't anything come up?" I looked over at him.

"Because I'm thirty-two years old and I don't waste my time on Facebook and Twitter."

I sighed. "And you really haven't spoken to her in six years?"

"Excuse me?" He looked over at me as we approached a red light. "I thought we just sorted this out in the bathroom."

"We did, but—" I cleared my throat. "You filed for a divorce, and it couldn't go through?"

"It takes *two* people to complete a divorce, Aubrey. Surely you know that."

"Yes, but…" I ignored the fact that he was clenching his jaw. "Wouldn't it be easier for someone like you to make it happen? Six years is a pretty long time to stay married to someone you claim you don't love anymore, so—"

"You'd be surprised at how well some people can spin a fucking lie to get what they want," he said, his voice cold. "My past isn't up for discussion."

"Ever?"

"*Ever*. It has nothing to do with you."

I leaned back in my seat, crossing my arms. "Are you ever going to tell me the reason why you left New York and moved to Durham?"

"No."

"Why not?"

"Because I don't have to." He steered the car into my apartment complex. "Because like I told you an hour ago, that part of my life never happened."

"I'm not going to tell anyone. I just—"

"*Stop it.*" He faced me as he stopped the car, and I could see a world of hurt in his eyes. It was the most vulnerable I'd ever seen him.

"I lost something very special in New York six years ago." There was regret in his voice. "Something I'll never fucking get back, something I've spent the last six years trying to forget, and if it's okay with you I'd like to make it to year *seven.*"

I opened my mouth to say sorry, but he continued talking.

"I'm not sure if I've made this apparent over the past six months or not," he said, "but I'm not the 'sit up and talk about my feelings' type. I'm not interested in deep conversations and just because I've fucked you more than once and can't seem to get you or your mouth off my mind, that doesn't entitle you to things I haven't told anyone else."

I immediately unbuckled my seatbelt and flung the door open, but he grabbed my wrist before I could get out.

"I meant what I said a few months ago, Aubrey…" He cupped my chin and tilted my head toward him. "You are my only friend in this city, but you have to understand that I'm not used to having friends. I'm not used to talking about personal shit, and I'm not going to start now."

Silence.

"If you're not going to open up to me, what incentive do I have to continue being your so-called *friend*?"

He said nothing for a few seconds, but then he smirked. "Get in my lap and let me show you."

"Is this a joke?"

"Am I laughing?"

"Do you really think you can just demand for me to have sex with you whenever you want?" I raised my eyebrow. "Especially since you just said you'll never be that open about your personal life?"

"Yes." He unbuckled his seat belt. "*Get in my lap.*"

"You know…" I looked down, noticing his cock slowly stiffening through his pants. "I've let a few things slide the past few times we've had sex, but I have to tell you…" I bit my lip as I

21

slipped out of the car. "I'm really not into the possessive caveman shit."

He narrowed his eyes at me as I grabbed my purse and stepped back.

"I think we need to give your cock a rest, don't you think?" I crossed my arms. "You have a pretty big hearing coming up next week. Don't you need to save all your energy so you can be better prepared?"

"Get back in the damn car, Aubrey..." His voice was strained.

"Are you begging me?"

"I'm *commanding* you."

"Did you not hear what I just said?"

He didn't answer. He reached for my hand, but I shut the door.

"I'll see you tomorrow, *Mr. Hamilton.*" I smiled and walked away.

liability (n.):

Legal responsibilities for one's acts or omissions.

A week later...

Andrew

There was only one thing in Durham that held no comparison to New York: Court. The lawyers in New York actually took their jobs seriously. They pored over their research all night, polished their defenses to perfection, and presented their cases with pride.

In Durham, "lawyers" didn't do shit, and in a moment like this—when I was listening to a young and inexperienced prosecutor embarrass herself, I almost missed those days.

Then again, I wasn't paying too much attention to the proceedings today. I was too busy thinking about Aubrey and how many times we'd fucked in my office this morning.

We'd said our usual, "Good morning Mr. Hamilton," "Hello, Miss Everhart" greetings and locked eyes as she set my coffee down. She'd opened her mouth to say something else, but the next thing I knew, my hands were in her hair and I was pulling her against my desk.

I was ruthlessly pounding into her from behind as I massaged her clit, and when she collapsed on my carpet, I'd spread her legs and devoured her pussy.

I was completely insatiable when it came to Aubrey, and being around her for more than five seconds was enough to send me over the edge.

There's no point in even counting how many times we've fucked anymore...

"As you can see..." The prosecutor's voice cut through my thoughts. "Ladies and gentlemen of the jury, all of the evidence that I've presented will prove—"

"Objection!" I'd had enough of this. "Your Honor, last time I checked, this was an *evidentiary hearing*, not a trial. Why is Ms. Kline being allowed to address a nonexistent jury?"

The judge took off her glasses. "Ms. Kline, as hesitant as I am to agree with Mr. Hamilton, he does have a point. Have you concluded with your presentation of evidence? Barring a closing statement to the jury?"

"I have, Your Honor," she said, puffing out her chest as if she'd just presented the case of the century.

"Mr. Hamilton..." The judge looked my way. "Do you care to surprise me today by refuting any of the evidence presented?"

"No, Your Honor." This hearing was a waste of time, and she knew it as well as I did.

"I see." She put on her glasses again. "Let the record show that while the prosecution has presented a compelling and rather large collection of evidence, it's this court's ruling that it is not enough to warrant a trial." She banged her gavel and stood up.

Ms. Kline walked over to me and held out her hand. "So, I'll file an appeal, get more evidence, and see you on this matter again soon, right?"

"Are you *asking* me or are you *telling* me?"

"Your client committed the highest degree of fraud, Mr. Hamilton." She crossed her arms. "Someone has to pay for that."

"No one ever will if you remain on top of it, will they?" I put my files in my briefcase. "I'll be waiting for your next move. And yes, you should get more evidence since the judge clearly ruled that what you had was not enough."

"So, that means I should appeal? Do you think I could win this thing?"

"I think you could go back to law school and fucking pay attention." I scoffed. "Either that, or do your clients a favor and find them a better lawyer."

"You mean someone like you?"

"There's *no one* like me." I slid a pair of shades over my eyes. "But anyone would be better than you."

"Are you always this rude to your opponents, Mr. Hamilton?" She cracked a smile. "I mean, I've heard stories, but you are really—"

"Really, what?"

"Intriguing." She stepped closer. "You are really intriguing."

I blinked and looked her over. If I'd met her on Date-Match she might've been worthy of one night, but I never mixed business with pleasure.

At least, I didn't used to.

"I'm not sure if you're seeing anyone or not," she said, lowering her voice, "but I think you and I have a lot in common."

"What exactly do we have in common, Miss Kline?"

"Well..." She stepped even closer and rubbed my shoulder. "We were both staring at each other during the hearing, we both have high profile careers, and we both have a passion for the law—a passion that could be transferred to *other things.*" She licked her lips. "Right?"

I stepped back. "Miss Kline, I was staring at you during the hearing because I was trying to comprehend how someone could show up to court and be so unprepared, unprofessional, and utterly annoying. We do both have high profile careers, but if you continue presenting cases like the one you presented today, I'll be interviewing you for a secretary position at my firm within the next six months." I ignored her gasp. "And if your passion for the law is *anything* like the way you fuck, then you and I have absolutely nothing in common."

"Did you..." She shook her head, stepping back as her face reddened. "Did you really just say that to me?"

"Did you really just proposition me for sex?"

"I was simply *probing*—seeing if you were interested in going out."

"I'm not," I said—noticing that I wasn't even the slightest bit aroused. "Am I free to leave the courtroom now or would you like to probe me for something else?"

"You are an asshole!" She spun around and grabbed her briefcase off the floor. "You know, for your clients' sake, I hope you're a lot nicer," she spat out as she left the room.

I wanted to tell her that I actually wasn't nicer to my clients. I didn't put up with bullshit from anyone, and since I hadn't lost a single case since moving to Durham, I didn't have to.

Looking at my watch, I figured I'd wait a few minutes before leaving. I didn't want to run into her in the parking lot, and since the remaining courts were adjourning for lunch, I figured I'd wait a while.

I stuffed my hands into my pocket and smiled at the feel of the lacy fabric that grazed my left hand. Pulling it out, I smiled at Aubrey's black thong from this morning.

I took my phone out of my briefcase to text her about it, but she'd emailed me first.

Subject: Wet Panty Fetish

I'm not sure if you've realized that I left my thong in your pocket yet, but I want you to know that I did it for your own good, and that your secret is safe with me.

Ever since you fucked me in the bathroom at the art gallery, I've noticed that you have a tendency to stare at my panties before taking them off.

You run your fingers across them, pull them off with your teeth, and then you stare at them again. I have no problem continuing to appease your panty fetish. I'm sure you place them over your face at night, so if you ever need more, feel free to let me know.

Aubrey

Subject: Re: Wet Panty Fetish
I did realize that you slipped your thong into my pocket this morning. I've noticed that you've done this all week.

Contrary to your unfounded and silly assumptions, I do not have a panty fetish and I do not sleep with them over my face at night. I do, however, have a new fetish for your pussy, and if you're interested in letting me sleep with THAT over my face at night, feel free to let me know.

Andrew

I waited for a response—watched my screen for several minutes, but then I realized it was Wednesday and she wouldn't see my email until later.

I made my way outside and slipped into my car. I didn't feel like going back to the firm—my case files were all up to date, and it was too early to go home.

Revving up my engine, I coasted down the street in search of a decent bar. As I was turning past the law school, I noticed Duke's dance hall across the street.

I wasn't sure what came over me, but I made a right turn and pulled into the parking lot. I followed the signs that read "Dance Studio" and parked in front.

There was a sign on the double doors of the auditorium that read "Private Rehearsals: Dancers Only," but I ignored it. I followed the faint sound of piano keys and opened the door to a colossal theater.

Bright lights shone directly on the stage, and dancers dressed in all white were spinning. Before I could come to my senses and make myself leave, I spotted Aubrey in the front.

Wearing the same feathered headband she'd worn at the art gallery, she was smiling wider than I'd ever seen her smile before—dancing as if no one else was in the room. There was a gleam in her eyes that I never saw while she was at GBH, and although I didn't know shit about ballet, it was clear that she was the best dancer onstage.

"Extend, Miss Everhart! *Extend!*" A grey haired man walked onto the stage, yelling. "More! More!"

She continued dancing—stretching her arms out further, extending her hands.

"No! No! NO!" The man stomped his foot. "Stop the music!"

The pianist immediately stopped and the director stepped in front of Aubrey.

"Do you know what the characteristics of the *white swan* are, Miss Everhart?" he asked.

"Yes."

"*Yes?*" He looked offended.

"Yes, Mr. Petrova." She stood still.

"If that's so, why don't you enlighten us all as to what those special characteristics are?"

"Light, airy, elegant—"

"Elegant!" He stomped his foot again. "The white swan is all about smooth, gentle movements…Her arms are well poised, graceful." He grabbed her elbow and pulled her forward. "Your arms are erratic, rough, and you're dancing like a pigeon on crack!"

Her cheeks reddened, but he continued.

"I want a swan, Miss Everhart, and if you're not up to the part—if your heart is elsewhere, like that other major you have, do me a favor and let me know so I can groom someone else for the role."

Silence.

"Let's try this again!" He stepped back. "On my count, start the song from the second stanza…"

I leaned back against the wall, watching Aubrey effortlessly dance again, as she made everyone else look like amateurs. I watched until I couldn't anymore, until her old director spotted my shadow and yelled at "the goddamn intruder" to leave.

———

Later that night, I walked into the kitchen and pulled out a bottle of bourbon—pouring myself a shot. It was two in the morning and I was beyond restless.

I hadn't been able to sleep since I came home and spotted a note from Ava on my door: *"I'm not leaving until we talk—Ava."*

I'd crumpled it and thrown it into the trash, wondering which person at GBH had been stupid enough to give out my address.

As I tossed back a shot, my phone rang.

"It's two in the morning," I hissed, holding it up to my ear.

"Um…" There was a slight pause. "May I speak to a…A Mr. Hamilton, please?"

"This is he. Did you *not* hear me say what time it is?"

"I'm sorry, Mr. Hamilton." She cleared her throat. "I'm Gloria Matter from the parole board in New York City. I'm sorry to call you so late, but I didn't want to turn in until I returned your inquiry from last week," she said. "The inmate you called about is no longer an inmate. She was released recently and is now on parole."

"I'm *aware* that she's on parole." I poured another drink. "However, I'm pretty sure leaving the state is a direct violation of those terms. Is New York soft on crime now? Do you let previous offenders roam the world as they please?"

"No sir, but she checked in with her officer this morning. We also checked her monitor the second we received your phone call so she's still in the state. I must warn you that we don't take too kindly to false reporting, Mr. Hamilton. If this was some type of—"

"I know what the fuck I saw." I seethed. "She was here." I hung up. I didn't care enough to think about Ava right now.

I headed into my bedroom and lay against the sheets, hoping this second round of alcohol would work better than the first.

I lay there for an hour, watching the seconds on my clock tick by, yet no sleep came and thoughts of Aubrey began to fill my mind. I was thinking about the things she'd told me when we we'd first met, things she'd told me about her sex life, and I had the sudden urge to hear her voice.

I rolled over and scrolled down to her name.

"Hello?" She answered on the first ring. "Andrew?"

"Why haven't you sucked a cock before?"

"*What*?" She gasped. "How about 'Good morning, Aubrey'? Are you awake?' How about asking those things first?"

"Hello, *Aubrey*." I rolled my eyes. "You're clearly awake, so I'll bypass that unnecessary question. Why haven't you sucked a cock before?"

She was silent.

"Do I need to drive to your apartment and make you answer the question *in person*?"

"Are you really in need of this information at three in the morning?"

"Desperately," I said. "Answer the question."

"It's just something I ever wanted to do." There were papers shuffling in the background. "One of the guys I used to date would ask me to do it to him from time to time—to reciprocate, but I just...I didn't like him enough to do it."

"Hmmm."

Silence.

We hadn't had an actual phone conversation since the last time we had phone sex, right before I found out her real name was Aubrey and not Alyssa.

"Were you thinking about me?" she asked.

"What?"

"Were you thinking about me?" she repeated. "You've never called me this late before. Are you lonely?"

"I'm horny."

She let out a soft laugh. "Would you like me to tell you what I'm wearing?"

"I already know what you're wearing."

"Oh, really?"

"Yes, really." I put a hand behind my head. "It's Wednesday, which means you had practice until midnight, which means you went home and showered and immediately put your feet in an ice tub without putting on any pajamas."

She sucked in a breath.

"And from the way you're breathing right now I take it you're still naked, and the reason you picked up my call on the first ring is because you want to touch yourself to the sound of my voice."

Another gap of silence.

"Am I wrong?" I asked.

"No…" Her voice was low. "I don't think you're horny right now though."

"Trust me. I am."

"Maybe, but I think you called me because you *like* me— because you want to hear my voice since we haven't talked on the phone in a while."

"I called you because my dick is hard and I want to make you cum over the phone."

She laughed again. "So, you don't like me?"

"I like your pussy."

"So, the white roses and the "He's just yelling at you because he knows you're the best. Don't let him get to you," note that was on the hood of my car today wasn't from you?"

I hung up.

retraction (n.):

The legal withdrawal of a promise or offer of contract.

Andrew

"How do you think we should proceed with the client, Harriet?" I leaned back in my chair the next night, dreading my "Let the Interns Help with One Case per Month" required hours.

"Um, Mr. Hamilton..." She twirled a strand of hair around her finger. "My name is Hannah."

"Same thing," I said. "How do you think we should proceed with this case?"

"We could put his ex-wife on the stand. She could vouch for his character."

"They were married for thirty days." I rolled my eyes and looked at the intern sitting next to her. "And that was ten years ago. Bob, what do you have?"

"It's...It's actually Bryan."

"It's whatever I say it is. What. Do. You. Have?"

"I was doing some research on his background and he apparently was reprimanded for breaking his university's firewall his senior year. We could start there and build a case around his past of anarchy..."

I sighed. "He's our client, Bryan. Why would we intentionally make him look bad?"

He blinked.

I turned toward the last intern in the room, a petite brunette. "What do you suggest?"

"You're not going to try and guess my name?" She smiled.

"I just realized that you weren't my janitor today. What do you have?"

"This." She slid a folder across the table. "If we're trying to prove that he wasn't in breach of his company's policies when he took out his initial shares, we could use this case as a reference."

I opened the folder, reading the first line of a case that was not only over a hundred years old, but it had been overturned by the Supreme Court decades ago.

"Did you all smoke the same drugs before your interviews?" I shook my head. "You're in *law school*. A few years away from potentially having someone's future in your hands and this is the type of shit you come up with?"

"With all due respect, Mr. Hamilton..." Bryan spoke up. "Is there even a right answer to this question? I mean...Is this one of those 'Ha-ha this was just a test to see how our minds work' things? Is there really an answer?"

"Yes." I stood up.

"Really? What is it?"

"It's go the fuck home." I started stacking my papers. "All of you. Right now."

"But—"

"Now." I glared at them, waiting until they all left the room.

The second I was alone I let out a sigh and sat down again. I was better off letting Jessica help me on this case. She didn't know shit about the law but I was sure that she would at least try.

"Mr. Hamilton, I—" Aubrey stepped into the room with a cup of coffee. "Where did everyone go?"

"Home." I took the cup from her, frustrated. "You're free to go, too."

"Are you ever going to formally give me my intern position back or am I forever stuck being your coffee and file organizer?"

"You're also in charge of taking phone calls. That's a responsibility you shouldn't take lightly."

"I'm serious…" She rolled her eyes. "As much as I enjoy having sex with you every morning with your coffee, I would like to go back to feeling like I actually have a purpose here."

"Fine." I took a sip from my cup. "Have you been keeping up with my current case?"

She nodded.

"Great," I said dryly. "How do you think I should proceed?"

"I think you need to first find the man who erased your client's identity."

"What? What are you talking about?"

She took a folder from her purse and set it in front of me. "My parents taught me how to research someone's background very, very well. That's the one thing I can credit them for." She flipped a few pages. "Your client has school records from his childhood—test scores, address changes, et cetera. There's a record of where he attended college, grad school—even a record of the time he broke into his school's firewall and got suspended for an entire semester. After that, there's a short failed marriage to some woman he met in Cabo, and a few founding records for his company. But after that—with the exception of these recent allegations, there's nothing."

I glanced at the pages.

"Don't you think that's odd?" She looked at me. "How you can google someone and nothing about them pops up? How you can search several databases for information and find entire decades are missing?"

I shut the folder. "It's slightly odd."

"*Slightly*?"

"Yes. Slightly. Is this all the evidence you have?"

"It's all the evidence you need." She stared into my eyes. "Find the guy who erased him, or find the guy who erased *you* and you might have yourself another win under your belt. If not—"

"*Aubrey...*"

"People don't just come out of nowhere, Andrew," she said. "You know that, I know that, and I'm pretty sure your client knows that."

"Now we're talking about *the client*?"

"There is no record of Andrew Hamilton in any of the state's registered lawyer databases."

"I'm not facing a trial."

"I called every law school in the state and pretended to be an alumna searching for a fellow alum and there was no record of an Andrew Hamilton getting his degree from any of them."

"Are you that obsessed with me?" He smirked.

"I did the same thing for the law schools in New York. That was a bit trickier, but the results were just the same. There was no record of you going to school during the years you would've been in attendance."

"And this affects you *how*?"

"You humiliated me when you found out I lied to you."

"I apologize."

"Don't." She shook her head. "You made me cry because you told me that I was a liar for hiding the truth and pretending to be someone I wasn't."

"I'm pretty sure I wouldn't be the only person to classify you as *a liar* after what you did."

"Yet, every day that I see you, every night that I talk to you on the phone, I'm no closer to getting to know anything about you." There was concern in her eyes. "It's always me talking about me, or you talking about abstract things that make up a blurry picture."

"It doesn't matter. I told you that I—"

"That you've never lied to me," she said. "I believe that, and for a moment I thought that you were always completely honest with me, but when I look back, you're only honest about what *you* want to talk about. Hence, the random appearance of *Mrs. Hamilton*, and—"

"I've told you about that already." I grabbed her hand and pulled her close to me. "So, I'm not going to waste my time rehashing shit I've already gone over with you."

"Just..."

"Look." I pressed my finger against her lips. "You're the only woman I've fucked regularly in six years."

"Am I supposed to be proud of that?"

I pulled her into my lap. "You're the only woman—only person actually, that I talk to outside of my hours at this office, the only woman I've ever fucked over the phone, the only woman who's been in my car, and the only woman who's lied to me and still gotten me to stay..."

She sighed, staring back at me.

"Now," I said, "if you don't mind, I'm going to fuck you in this chair. And when we're done, I'll kindly show you how to research someone the right way, because contrary to what you think, my client does have a background."

"No, I double checked everything and I—"

I pressed my lips against hers. "*After* I fuck you."

consent (n.):

A voluntary agreement to another's proposition.

Aubrey

Subject: New York / Your Panties
For the record, I did go to law school in NYC. I was the valedictorian of my class.

—Andrew

PS—If you stash one more pair of your wet panties/"For your fetish" notes in my desk drawer, I'm going to assume that you *do* want me to sleep with your pussy over my face. My tongue has been aching to do that since I first "met" you so there's no need for unnecessary hints...

"Aubrey?" My mother's voice took the smile right off of my face. "Aubrey, were you listening to your father just now?"

"No, I'm sorry." I sighed, dreading that I was still sitting at a dinner with them.

They'd called me the second my rehearsal was over and demanded that I drive home so we could all ride to our "favorite" restaurant together. It was where all their country club friends ate regularly, and I knew they just wanted to come here to assert our seemingly perfect family image.

"Are you listening now?" My father raised his eyebrow.

"Yes…"

"We brought you here so we could tell you that I'm running for governor in the next election," he said.

"Do you want my vote?"

"Ugh, Aubrey." My mother huffed and snapped her fingers for the waiter. "This is one of the happiest moments of your life."

"No…" I shook my head. "I'm pretty sure it *isn't.*"

"All those years of hard work, building our firm to be one of the most impeccable in the city," she said as she looked into my father's eyes, "it's about to payoff in a huge way. We already have a few verbal commitments for the campaign's budget, and since we're going in on the same side as the incumbent—"

"You have a really good chance of being governor." I cut her off. "Congratulations, Dad."

He reached over the table and squeezed my hand.

My mother couldn't seem to shut up. "We'll have to take new family photos—stocks, you know? Photos we can give to the press for their write-ups, so you'll have to wear your hair in something other than that ballerina thing."

"It's a *bun.*"

"It's an eyesore."

"*Margaret…*" My father chided. "It's not an eyesore. It's just—"

"It's just *what?*" I looked back and forth between them.

"It's important for us to look like a cohesive All-American unit on the campaign trail." My mother took a glass of wine from the waiter and waited for him to step away. "We may have to make some stops together as a family."

"You're running for *governor*, not President, and what twenty-something do you know travels with her parents during a campaign just for photo-ops?"

"Our opponent has twenty year old twins who are home-schooled," she said. "They travel to third world countries every summer to help the poor and I'm pretty sure they're going to be at every stop on the campaign trail."

I snorted. "Why are you trying to compete with genuine people? Don't you think they're the type that deserve to win?"

"Aubrey, this is serious." My dad looked upset. "This has been a dream of mine for a very long time and we want to make sure that nothing stands in the way."

The two of them exchanged glances and I raised my eyebrow. "Nothing like *what*?" I asked.

"Okay…" My mother lowered her voice and looked over her shoulder before speaking. "We need to know if there are any skeletons in your closet—any pictures on social media that make you look like a party girl, any ex-boyfriends or sexual partners that you may have dealt with, or *anything* that would make us look like bad parents."

"You *are* bad parents."

"Stop it, Aubrey." My father gripped my hand and squeezed it hard. "The two of us have given you everything you could've ever wanted growing up and all we're asking for is a small sacrifice from you."

"I don't have any skeletons in my closet." I gritted my teeth.

"Good." My mother put on her fake smile. "Then, when you pull out of school for your senior year to help us on the trail, it won't look suspicious. We've already spoken to your department chair about online classes and they are, in fact, offered. For the ones that aren't, you'll have to show up to campus to take those, but they make special considerations for students with circumstances such as yours so—"

"No." I cut her off. "No, thank you."

"This isn't up for discussion, Aubrey. This is for the benefit of—"

"Dad's *dream*, right?" I tried not to lose it. "Because he's the only person in this family who has a dream?"

"Yes," my mother said through smiling teeth. "We're talking about *real* dreams, Aubrey. Not 'no-chance-in-hell' and failed ones."

"Excuse me?!" I stood up. "You want to talk about *failed dreams* when the two of you have failed more than anyone I know at the expense of your own daughter?" There were tears in my eyes.

"Aubrey, sit back down." She grabbed my hand. "Let's not make a scene."

"*Let's!*" I snatched my hand away. "Let's discuss how I'm twenty fucking two and I'm *a junior* in college when I should already be a graduate! Shall we? Can you explain why that is?"

My father's face reddened and he motioned for me to sit down, but I stood my ground.

My mother clutched her pearls. "Aubrey…We did what was best at the time, and even though switching school systems twice in two years was unfortunate, it made you who you are today. Now, the campaign won't start until—"

"I don't care when the hell it starts. I'm not going on a pointless campaign trail, and I'm not taking any of my classes online because guess what?" I could feel my blood boiling. "You can't learn fucking ballet *online!*"

The restaurant was now silent.

"You two are beyond selfish and you don't even know it." I shook my head. "I'm voting for the other guy." I stormed off amidst gasps and whispers from the other tables—slightly content that my parents' picture perfect image had been publicly scratched a bit.

"Your number, Miss?" The valet said to me as I stepped outside.

"My what?"

"Your number?" He tilted his head to the side. "For your car?"

Shit…I sighed and looked over my shoulder.

Patrons were pointing in my direction and I couldn't bear to go back inside just because I didn't have a ride home.

I considered calling a cab, but I knew that was pointless. It would take forever to get here, and I could probably walk to my apartment faster than they would arrive.

There was a bus stop a mile or so down, but I only had a credit card. I doubted Andrew would come get me, but I decided to give it a try.

Subject: A Ride.
I really need a favor...
—Aubrey

Subject: Re: A Ride
Wanting to take a ride on my cock in the middle of the day shouldn't be considered a "favor" at this point.
—Andrew

Subject: Re: Re: A Ride
I'm not talking about your dick. I'm talking about your car...Would you be able to pick me up right now? I was at a dinner with my parents but it didn't end well...and I don't have my car.
If you can't, I'll understand.
—Aubrey

Subject: Re: Re: Re: A Ride
Where are you?
—Andrew

Half an hour later, he pulled into the country club's driveway.

I slipped into his car before he could even park—not looking back at the snooty members who were probably whispering and wondering about what had happened between me and my parents.

"I'm taking you home, right?" he asked as he pulled off.

"No..."

He looked over at me. "Am I taking you to GBH?"

"If you want. Just not to my apartment." I paused. "I'm sure my parents will stop by there after dinner and try to talk to me so..."

"Have you eaten?"

"Lost my appetite..." I said softly, then I smiled. "But if you're interested in taking me on a date right now, I'm not opposed to that."

"Why would I take you on *a date*?"

"Because you owe me one."

"Since when?"

"You once said that you would take me out if we ever met in person, and you haven't done it yet."

We approached a stoplight and he turned to face me.

"If I was even vaguely interested in taking you out right now—which *I'm not*, where the hell would I take you if you've already eaten dinner?"

"Surprise me." I shrugged and leaned against the glass—shutting my eyes. I could picture him staring at me, giving me that "You're out of your damn mind" look, and as he steered the car back onto the street, I smiled—hoping that this would be the start of us going out regularly.

I was dreaming of him kissing me in the gallery room again when I felt him gently shaking my shoulder.

"Aubrey..." he whispered. "Aubrey, wake up."

I lifted my head and looked outside my window. There were lush plants and a massive glass paned building—an executive condo. My heart skipped a beat because I knew he'd never taken a woman to his place before, and I was happy that I would be the first.

I looked over at him, ready to say something, but then I saw him fiddling with a green parking pass and I looked out the front window—seeing where we really were.

Outside of a Hilton hotel.

"Your idea of taking me on a date is bringing me to *a hotel?*"

"It's more about fucking you in the hotel."

"Andrew, this is where you take all your other dates..."

"And?"

My heart sank. "Do you not see why bringing me here would hurt my feelings?"

"Would you prefer the *Marriott?*"

I blinked.

"They don't have the same standard of room service," he said, "but if that's what you prefer—"

"Just take me home—*right now.*" My voice cracked and I leaned against the window, shutting my eyes again. "I'll deal with my parents..."

———

I woke up on a plush leather couch, tucked underneath a soft black blanket.

Sitting up, I saw that my shoes had been taken off and placed in a rack on the other side of the room. A tray of fresh fruit and chocolates were sitting on the small table in front of me, and there was a bottle of wine sitting next to two stemmed glasses.

The room looked as if it'd been plucked from a magazine: silk white draperies, taupe walls, and portraits framed in silver. One of those portraits was of a fucking hotel, making it clear exactly where I was.

I immediately tossed the blanket off—ready to find Andrew and yell at him for bringing me here against my wishes. I walked down the hallway, slowly noticing that the pictures hanging on the wall were of him.

In one picture, he was standing on a beach, looking off into the distance. In another he was standing in front of a NYC cab, and in another he was lying against a city park bench.

He was young in all of these photos—his eyes held a more boyish charm, and if I wasn't mistaken, he looked happy. Extremely happy.

In between all of the larger photos, were small wooden blocks in the shape of an entwined "E" and "H." At first I thought that the "A" for Andrew's first name was simply missing, that one of the pieces would bear it, but that wasn't the case: In the last frame at the end of the hall there was a photo of a huge "E" and "H" that were solely compiled of pictures of New York.

"E" and "H"?

I continued walking down the hallway, smiling at the more "esteemed" photos he'd hung of himself. I stopped when I heard the sound of running water and followed it into a massive bedroom.

Everything was cloaked in black—the sheets that covered the king sized bed, the long silk curtains that hung over the balcony's French doors, and the plush rug that sat atop his polished wooden floors.

I walked over to his armoire and pulled out the first drawer.

"What are you doing?" Andrew was standing right behind me.

"I was..." I stalled as he wrapped an arm around my waist. "I was looking through your stuff."

"Looking for anything *particular*?" He kissed the shell of my ear from behind.

"I'm looking for where you keep all my panties."

He let out a low laugh. "They're all next to my bed." He slid his hand underneath my skirt and stalled once his fingers reached my bare pussy. "Since you're not wearing any, do I need to give them back to you?"

I rolled my eyes and he let me go.

"Is this better than a hotel room?" he asked.

"Depends." I turned around. "How many other women have you had here?"

"None."

"None?" I couldn't believe that. "In *six years*?"

"I like to keep my fucking life separate from my home life." He clasped my hand.

"So, I'm the exception to the rule?"

He didn't answer. He simply led me across the bedroom and into an all-white en-suite where the water from the shower was still running.

"I've been waiting for you to wake up…" He looked down at me.

"Because you want to watch movies together?"

"Because I want to fuck you in the shower." He pushed my back against the wall and looked into my eyes. "Because I want to fuck you all night."

I moaned as he wedged his knee between my thighs and pulled my shirt over my head. He slipped his hand behind my back to unclasp my bra, and as it fell to the floor he trailed his tongue across my nipples.

"Take off your skirt…" He backed away from me.

My hands went to my zipper, but my eyes stayed glued on him as he started to undress himself.

I'd fucked him numerous times in his office, recklessly rode his cock time and time again, but I'd never seen him completely naked.

He pulled his white V-neck shirt over his head and tossed it into the corner—exposing a set of chiseled abs and a small cursive tattoo that was etched onto his chest.

I tried to read what the words said, but then he unfastened the drawstring of his black lounge pants and let them fall to the floor.

I could see that his cock was hard through his briefs, and I waited for him to take them off, but he walked back over to me.

Grabbing my hand, he placed it against his waistline. "Take them off of me."

I slipped my thumb underneath the elastic, but he stopped me.

"With *your mouth.*"

My eyes widened as I looked up at him, seeing the sexy smirk on his face.

I bent down slightly and trailed kisses across his waist—hearing him take in a sharp breath as his hands slipped into my hair.

I gripped his thighs for balance and tugged at the hem of his briefs with my teeth. Pulling the fabric down a few inches, I used my fingers to move them further, but he pulled me back by my hair.

"Only your mouth." He warned.

I gave him a look of understanding and he let me go. I once again grabbed the briefs with my teeth and slowly slid them down his legs.

I looked up and saw that his cock was standing at attention, rock hard and ready for my pussy like always, and from the look in his eyes, I knew he was going to pull me up and fuck me against the wall.

Before he could get the chance, I sat up on my knees and gripped his cock with my hand. I pressed my lips against it—trailing my tongue across every thick inch. I wrapped my mouth around his tip and slowly massaged it with my tongue.

"Aubrey…" He threaded his fingers through my hair and looked down at me. "What are you doing?"

"I'm…" I felt my cheeks heating. "I'm sucking your cock."

He blinked, letting a slow smile spread across his face. "You're not sucking my cock…You're *kissing* it."

"I was getting to that part. I was trying to do it like…" I shook my head and stood up, completely embarrassed. "Never mind."

"You were trying to do it like *what?*" he whispered against my lips. I shook my head again and he looked into my eyes. "You don't need to watch anybody else to learn. *I'll* teach you..."

Still smiling, he grabbed my hand and pulled me into the shower. He pressed his chest against mine and slipped a finger into my mouth as the water ran over us. "Is this as wide as you can open for me?"

I blinked, nodding.

"You're going to have to open a lot wider than that if my cock is going to fit into your mouth..." He sat down on the small wet bench behind him and motioned for me to bend low.

The water streams from above lashed against my back as I got down on my knees.

"Lick your lips," he commanded, and I obliged—feeling completely out of my zone.

I leaned forward, assuming that I was supposed to take him into my mouth now, but he stopped me.

"Make it wet."

"*What?*"

"Put your mouth on my cock and *wet it.*"

Hesitant, I pressed my lips against his dick and slid my tongue across his shaft. I was swirling it against him slowly, but then he pulled my head up.

"You're being too gentle," he said. "I don't need you to be a fucking lady right now..."

"I—"

"I need you to be aggressive, greedy, and *sloppy* because I'm not going to be gentle when I'm devouring you." He gently pushed my head down and spread his legs a little further. "Massage my balls with your hand..."

I immediately cupped them, rubbing them against each other.

"A little harder..." His breathing slowed and I picked up the pace of my fingers.

"Now," he whispered. "Open your mouth as wide as it can go, and take my cock as deep as you can…"

I opened my mouth and took in the first few inches easily as he threaded a few fingers through my hair.

"*Keep your eyes on me.*" He looked somewhat impressed. "You don't have to take all of it right now…" He used my shoulders to push me back and then forward. "Keep easing it in and out of your mouth just like this…"

Groaning, he stared at me with pure lust in his eyes, and then he whispered. "Suck me deeper…"

I followed his command and he groaned even louder. I could see the muscles in his legs tensing as my mouth covered over half of his cock. I was starting to feel a little bolder, slightly more confident, so I took in a little bit more of him.

"*Fuck…*" He breathed.

I used my free hand to cover the part of his cock that wasn't in my mouth, and massaged it the same way I was massaging his balls—soft but aggressive.

He started to tug at my hair, begging me to take more of him into my mouth. "Take all of it…"

Feeling as if I was now in control, I denied his request, and sped up my rhythm—bobbing my head up and down.

"*Aubrey…*" His words were strained.

I took him a little deeper—wrapping my lips around him a little tighter, but I didn't go all the way.

"*Aubrey…*" he said again, sounding desperate.

I wasn't paying his words any attention. I was loving the way his cock felt inside my mouth, loving the way my tongue was commanding him and making him react.

"*Stop.*" He yanked me back by my hair and glared at me. "Take all of my cock into your fucking mouth right now."

I slid my mouth over him and leaned forward all the way—not stopping until it touched the back of my throat.

Andrew briefly shut his eyes and sighed. Then he opened them again and spoke firmly. "I need you to let me cum in your mouth…" His voice was raspy. "And I need you to swallow every fucking drop…"

I gripped his knees and sucked him faster and faster, and his cock began to throb in my mouth. I could feel it pulsating, constricting, and as he leaned back and finally let go I felt spurts of warmness slipping down my throat.

His cum was salty and thick, and I honestly loved the taste of it. As the last drop landed into my mouth, I looked into his eyes and he looked back at me. The expression on his face was one of pure satisfaction and awe, and I was more turned on than I'd ever been in my life.

He stood—pulling me with him, and pressed his lips against mine. "That was fucking perfect." He turned off the water and led me out of the shower and back into his bedroom—not bothering to dry me off.

He grabbed me by my waist and tossed me onto the bed. "Spread your legs."

I let my legs fall apart and he climbed on top of me. Crashing his lips against mine, he sucked my bottom lip into his mouth.

I could feel the tip of his cock rubbing against my pussy and I lifted my hips—encouraging him to fuck me.

After being with him in the shower, I didn't want to do much foreplay and I didn't want to talk.

I just wanted to be fucked. Now.

His hands caressed my breasts and I pushed them away. "Fuck me, Andrew."

"I am."

"*Now*."

He smiled at me, looking as if he wanted to say something smart, but he leaned over and reached into his nightstand for a condom.

WHITNEY G.

He quickly slipped it on and entered me in one full stroke, causing me to moan in pleasure.

"Ahhhh…" I reached up and grabbed his hair as his cock pounded into me relentlessly. I was sure I'd never get tired of him fucking me, each time was better than the last.

I shut my eyes as he buried his head in my neck, as he whispered how "fucking good" I felt. Small tremors started building inside of me, and as much as I wanted this to last a little longer, I wouldn't be able to hold on.

"Andrewww…" I said his name as my hips started to jerk and my orgasm took over me. I screamed, falling back onto the pillows, and he collapsed on top of me seconds later.

We both lay there, entwined in each other for a long time—not saying a word. When I finally found the energy to speak, I cleared my throat. "Are you going to sleep inside of me all night?"

"Of course not." He pulled out of me, immediately making me miss the feel of him. He walked over to his closet, tossing the condom away.

"What are you doing?" I sat up.

"Getting dressed."

"For what?"

"So I can take you home." He slipped into a pair of pants. "And so I can go to sleep." He put on a shirt, and then he looked over at me. "How long do you think it'll take you to get ready?"

"I don't need you to take me home." I shook my head. "I want to stay here."

"Here?" he looked utterly confused.

"Yes, *here.*"

"As in *overnight?*"

I nodded, and he stood there staring at me as if I'd just asked him to do the unthinkable. The look he was giving me was one of anguish, regret, and for a second I almost felt bad about suggesting it.

"Aubrey, I don't…" He sighed. "I've never let someone spend the night."

"Then let me be your first…"

He continued staring at me, tapping his chin, and then he walked over to his closet and grabbed a set of white pajamas.

"You can sleep in these…" He held them out for me.

I reached out to take them but he shook his head.

"Stand up."

I slid off the bed and stood in front of him.

He took his time helping me into the button up shirt—kissing every inch of my exposed skin until he reached the top button, and when he was finished he kissed my lips.

I expected him to hold out the pants next, but he tossed them across the room. "Get in the bed."

Smiling, I slipped underneath the sheets as he hit the lights.

He joined me in bed seconds later, pulling me against his chest.

"Are you happy?" he whispered.

"Yes…"

"Are you sure? Is there anything else outside of my comfort zone that you'd like me to do for you tonight?"

"Not tonight, but you could make me breakfast in the morning."

"You're pushing it…"

"Just in case you change your mind, I would like Belgian waffles, bacon, sliced strawberries, and orange juice."

"Unless you want to eat all of those things off of my cock, it's not happening." He pinched my ass. "Go to sleep, Aubrey."

———

In the morning, I opened my eyes and realized I was alone in Andrew's bed. I looked over at where he'd been sleeping and spotted a note on GBH stationery:

Had to run to the office to meet a new client. I'll be back to take you home.

PS—Feel free to take your panty collection home with you.

—Andrew

I slipped out of bed, ready to explore more of his condo, but there was a sudden loud knock at the door. I rushed over and twisted the knob, expecting to see Andrew, but it was a man dressed in all black.

"Um hello?" I tried not to look too confused.

"Are you Aubrey Everhart?"

"Yes..."

"Great." He handed me a white bag. "Gourmet waffles, bacon, sliced strawberries, and orange juice, right?"

denial (n.):

A statement in the defendant's answer to a complaint in
a lawsuit that an allegation (claim of fact) is not true.

A few days later...

Andrew

I was officially out of my damn mind.
I was in my bathtub, and Aubrey was sitting on top of me—panting as she came down from another orgasm.

She was spending the night at my condo for the third time
this week, and it was pointless to even pretend like I minded.

I wasn't sure what the hell was happening, but she'd definitely
gotten to me. She was infiltrating my every thought, and no matter
what I did to try and come back to my senses—to remind myself
that this could only be temporary, she slipped deeper into my life.

"Why are you so quiet tonight?" she asked.

"I'm not allowed to think?"

"Not when a naked woman is in your lap."

"I was giving her a chance to relax." I slid my hands underneath her thighs. "What unnecessary bullshit do you want to talk
about today?"

"It's not *unnecessary*," she said. "It's about your family."

"What about my family?"

"Are they still in New York?"

I prevented myself from clenching my jaw. "I don't know."

"You *don't know*?" She raised her eyebrow. "What do you mean you don't know? Are you estranged from them?"

"No..." I sighed. "I just don't have any parents."

She tilted her head to the side. "Then why do I remember you telling me a story about your mom the first month that we met?"

"What *story*?"

"The story about Central Park and ice cream." She looked into my eyes, as if she were expecting me to say something. "You said she took you to some children's fair, I think? It was something that happened every Saturday. But the one you remembered most happened when it was raining and she still took you, and you stood in line for an hour just to get a scoop of vanilla."

I blinked.

"Is that story not right? Am I mixing it up with something else?"

"No," I said. "That's right...But I haven't seen her since."

"Oh..." She looked down. "I'm sorry."

"Don't be." I trailed a finger across her lips. "I turned out just fine."

"Can I ask you a few more things?"

"You have a daily question quota starting today."

She rolled her eyes. "What do all the "E" and "H" pictures in your hallway stand for?"

I felt a sudden ache in my chest. "*Nothing*."

"If you hate New York so much and you don't like talking about your past or *what you lost* six years ago, why do you have so many mementos hanging on your walls?"

"Aubrey..."

"Okay, forget that question. And the Latin quote across your heart? What does it mean?"

"Lie about one thing, lie about it all." I kissed her lips before she could ask me anything else. I was starting to wonder why she hadn't wanted to be a damn journalist instead of a ballerina.

"It's your turn," she said softly. "You can ask *me* questions now."

"I'd rather fuck you again." I lifted her with me as I stood up and helped her out of the bath tub.

We both dried off and went into my bedroom. Just as I was pulling her against me, my doorbell rang.

I sighed. "Dinner's early." I slipped into a pair of lounge pants and a T-shirt and headed to the door with my credit card.

The second I opened it, I was confronted with the sight of the last person on earth I wanted to see. *Ava.*

"Don't you dare fucking slam it on me this time," she hissed. "We need to talk."

"We don't need to talk about shit." I stepped outside and shut the door behind me. "How many times do I have to tell you that you're not wanted here?"

"As many times as it'll take you to actually believe it, which you don't." She scoffed. "Ask me why I came to Durham to see you, *Mr. Hamilton*. Appease me and I'll finally go the hell away."

"You're going the hell away regardless," I said flatly. "I really don't give a fuck why you came here."

"Not even if it's to sign the divorce papers?"

"You could've sent that shit in the mail." I gritted my teeth. "And since I'm sure you're running out of loopholes for contesting it, I'm willing to wait until all your options run out. I'm sure your lawyers will drop you as soon as they find out what *type* of client you are."

"All I'm asking for is ten thousand a month."

"Go ask the man who was fucking you in our bedroom while I was at work." I glared at her, livid. "Or better yet, ask the judge you only "fucked for a favor," or hey, if you're up to it, fuck my former best friend. Sleeping with him always seemed to make you feel better, right?"

"You weren't *Mr. Perfect* either."

"I never fucking *cheated* on you, and I never *lied* to you."

Silence.

"Five thousand a month," she said.

"Go fuck yourself, Ava."

"You know I *never* give up," she said, her eyes widened as I stepped back inside my apartment. "I *always* get what I want."

"*So do I.*" I slammed the door in her face, feeling my heart palpitating, feeling the onset of ugly memories all over again.

Rain. New York. Heartbreak.

Complete and utter heartbreak.

Seeing Ava in person again—hearing her manipulative voice and feeling those familiar pangs in my chest, immediately made me realize that I couldn't make the same mistake again.

Aubrey was already asking questions, trying to dig her way into my life as much as she could—thinking that if she stayed around long enough that we would work out together. But I knew that would never happen, not after seeing Ava and knowing just how far she would go to ruin me all over again.

I was officially done with this monogamous game we'd been playing for the past couple weeks. It was quite fun—*different*, but since Aubrey could never be mine and I could never be hers, it was quite fucking pointless, too.

I headed back into my bedroom and saw Aubrey smiling as she settled into the bed.

"Where's the dinner?" she asked tilting her head to the side. "Did you leave it at the door?"

"*No.*" I shook my head and started packing up her things, stuffing them all into her purse.

"What are you doing?" she asked.

"You can't stay the night."

"Okay…" She stood up. "Did something just happen? Do you want to talk about—"

"I don't want to talk about anything else with you." I hissed. "I just want to take you the hell home."

"What?" She looked confused. "What's wrong with you? Why are you—"

"Make sure you get all of your shit out of my bathroom. You won't be coming back here again."

"Why not?"

"Because I need to start fucking someone else." I picked up her headband. "I think I've spent more than enough time with you, don't you think?"

"*Andrew*..." Her face fell. "Where is all of this coming from?"

"The same place it was always coming from. You lied to me once, you'll lie again."

"I thought we were over that."

"Maybe *you* were, but I wasn't."

"What are you saying?"

"I'm saying that you need to get all of your things so I can take you home, and from here on out, you are my intern and I am your boss. You will forever be Miss Everhart to me, and to you I'll be Mr. Hamilton."

"*Andrew*..."

"*Mr. Fucking. Hamilton.*"

She rushed over to me and snatched her things, letting a few tears escape her eyes. "Fuck you. FUCK. YOU. This is the last time you'll ever pull this hot and cold shit on me." She stormed out of my apartment, slamming the door behind her.

I sighed and felt an immediate pang of guilt in my chest, but I knew it was the right thing to do. It was either cut this bullshit off now, or be responsible for breaking her heart later.

I stepped onto the balcony and lit a cigar—looking up at the moonless sky. Even though I felt bad for ending things so abruptly, for putting her out with no explanation, I needed to get back to who the hell I was and fast before I fucked up and put my heart on the line again...

closing argument (n.):

The final argument by an attorney on behalf of his/her client after all evidence has been produced for both sides.

Andrew (Well...Back then, you would've called me "Liam A. Henderson")

Six years ago
New York

There's something about this city that makes me believe again. It's the hopefulness in the air, the flashing lights that shine brighter than anywhere else, and the dreamers who fill the streets day after day—unwilling to give up on their failures until they finally win. There's no other city like it, and there's nothing more alluring outside these state lines—nothing that will ever make me leave.

As the sun sets in the distance, I wrap my arm around my wife's waist. We're standing against the railing of the Brooklyn Bridge—smiling because I just added another high profile client to my firm.

"You think one day the papers will actually tell the truth about your first case?" She looked up at me with her light green eyes. "Or do you think they'll keep brushing it under the rug?"

"Brushing it under the rug." I sigh. "I highly doubt the government wants people knowing that a kid straight out of law school uncovered a conspiracy. It's an insult to their organization."

"So, you're fine being reduced to a random Jeopardy question that'll happen ten years from now? 'I'll take lawyers who never got credit for two hundred, Alex.' You're fine with that?"

"Why shouldn't I be?" I kiss her forehead. "I didn't need the papers to print my name to get clients. People knew, that's how they found me."

"You should be so much bigger than what you are..." She shakes her head, whispering, "Your name should be plastered across every billboard in the city. Fucking assholes..."

Smiling, I tighten my grip around her waist and start the walk back to our car. Out of all the people that have come in and out of my life, Ava Sanchez has been the one constant.

She's the only woman I've ever loved, and ever since the day I made her mine at our wedding three years ago, I swore that would never change.

"I was also thinking," she says as she slips into the passenger seat, "that maybe me, you, and your partner Kevin could go out to a singles' mixer next weekend."

"Why would we go to a singles mixer?"

"It's more so for Kevin...He needs to get his own life. I'm tired of him hanging around us all the time. It's bad enough that we all work at your firm together, but do we *have* to spend our every waking moment together, too?"

Laughing, I drive down the city streets and home to the colossal brownstone we share. (It was the first purchase I'd made after winning the "case that never was," and Ava had insisted that I buy the most expensive one.)

"Because you fucking deserve it," she'd said. "And you never treat yourself to anything nice...That's what I don't understand about you, Liam. You're such a nice guy to everyone but yourself..."

I park our car in front of our home and immediately step out to open her door. As usual, Ava whispers, "I bet she'll scream for you first," as I walk her up the steps.

The second we walk inside, that familiar sweet voice rings out across the room.

"*Daddyyyyy!*"

I let go of Ava's hand and stoop low so my daughter—*Emma Henderson*, can run into my arms. She's the best part of my day, the best part of my life, and seeing her always brings an unbreakable smile to my face.

I kiss her forehead as she incoherently babbles about her day with the babysitter, and I smile as her blue eyes stare into mine.

I'm unaware of it now—I'm too blind and happy to see it, but in the months to come, my life will unravel so rapidly and unexpectedly that I'll wish I never existed. The lies that come to the light will be so devastating and crushing that my entire life will crumble around me. But the worst part, the part that will break me, is not knowing that this present moment with my 'daughter' will be the last good memory of New York I'll ever have…

end of episode two

acknowledgments

First and foremost, thank you Tamisha Draper for being the amazing and wonderful powerhouse that you are. You answer my endless phone calls (much to your husband's dismay lol), read my books over and over again, and even force me to sit down and write sex scenes when I say things like, "Would the readers really hate me if I just faded all of these sex scenes to black? No, really. Would they? They'd still love me, right?"

I don't know of anyone who would willingly work so tirelessly—anyone who would spend fifty plus hours a week working on a career that is not her own, in exchange for next to nothing...

I'm actually crying while writing this because I honestly don't deserve to have a friend as great as you. You go above and beyond with every single book I write, and you push me to make sure that each one is ten times better than the last. (If I ever make it, I swear I will find the best way to pay you back. I fucking promise.)

Thank you to all of my blogger friends that I've made so far— Bobbie Jo Malone Kirby (Why do you pick such EMOTIONAL books?! lol), Kimberly Kimball, Stephanie Locke, Lisa Pantano Kane, Michelle Kannan, and COUNTLESS more! (If I left someone out, I am sooo sorry! And hey, I self-published this, so I can easily re-upload it with your name here lol...Seriously though, I can...)

Thank you to Evelyn Guy for the final proofreading work...I noticed you didn't write much in the sex scene parts...LOL

Thank you to my mother, Lafrancine Maria, for letting me read this book to you aloud. Can't wait to see your face when I read book 3!!!

Last and NEVER EVER least, thank you to the best readers in the world! I really do love you more than you'll ever know!! (Or, as you know me to say, I. Fucking. Love. You.) So, question. How do you like Andrew? Do you think he gives Jonathan Statham a run for his money? LOL

Fucking Love You,

Whit

letter to the reader

Dear Incredible Reader,

Thank you so much for taking time out of your life to read this book! I hope you were thoroughly entertained and enjoyed reading it as much as I enjoyed writing it.

If you have any extra time, PLEASE leave a review on amazon. com, B&N.com, goodreads.com, OR send me an email (whitgbooks@gmail.com) so I can personally thank you :-)

I'm forever grateful for you and your time, and I hope to be re-invited to your bookshelf with my next release.

Love,

Whitney Gracia Williams

more works by whitney gracia williams:

Twisted Love (*2014*)
Wasted Love (*Winter 2014*)
Reasonable Doubt #1-3 (2014)
My Last Resolution: A Novella (January 2014)
Mid Life Love: At Last (October 2013)
Mid-Life Love (*June 2013*)
Final Take (Jilted Bride Series)
Take Three* (Jilted Bride Series)
Take Two* (Jilted Bride Series)
Captain of My Soul: A Memoir (*July 2009*)

*These books were pulled from publication, but will be re-released in the coming months.

You can keep up with Whitney and the travels of her non-matching socks at http://www.whitneygracia.com

To be a part of the mailing list and be notified of release dates and special offers, email whitgbooks@gmail.com with "Mailing List" in the subject heading.

Made in the USA
Monee, IL
25 April 2022